THE
INVADERS

It stopped about a metre in front of us, and hovered on a level with our faces.

Then the globe started moving back. It went slowly at first, picked up speed, flashed down the High Street, flew over the roofs, and disappeared from sight.

Kelly and Luke are staying with their grandparents. Nothing exciting ever happens, they keep telling themselves. This time, though, they wake up to find that not only have their grandparents disappeared, but so has the rest of the village population. Kelly and Luke are completely alone – apart from a black, menacing object coming straight towards them . . .

Thriller Firsts is an exciting series of fast-paced stories especially for younger readers of the eight to ten age group. With clear, straightforward text and plenty of illustrations, readers are sure to be gripped.

Tony Bradman is the author of many books for children, among them *One Nil*, *Gerbil Crazy*, the *Bluebeards* series and *Dilly the Dinosaur*. He lives in London with his wife and three children.

Other titles in the series

THRILLER FIRSTS

THE INVADERS

Tony Bradman

Illustrated by Mark Burgess

BLACKIE CHILDREN'S BOOKS

For Sally, who saved my bacon – again

BLACKIE CHILDREN'S BOOKS

Published by the Penguin Group
Penguin Books Ltd, 27 Wrights Lane, London W8 5TZ, England
Penguin Books USA Inc., 375 Hudson Street, New York, New York 10014, USA
Penguin Books Australia Ltd, Ringwood, Victoria, Australia
Penguin Books Canada Ltd, 10 Alcorn Avenue, Toronto, Ontario, Canada M4V 3B2
Penguin Books (NZ) Ltd, 182–190 Wairau Road, Auckland 10, New Zealand

Penguin Books Ltd, Registered Offices: Harmondsworth, Middlesex, England

First published 1993
1 3 5 7 9 10 8 6 4 2
First edition

Filmset in 14/18pt Linotype Baskerville
by Rowland Phototypesetting Ltd,
Bury St Edmunds, Suffolk
Printed in Great Britain by
Butler and Tanner Ltd, Frome, Somerset

A CIP catalogue record for this book is available from the British Library

ISBN 0–216–94024–9

Contents

Author's Note

The War of the Worlds is one of my favourite science fiction stories. It was written by H. G. Wells, who grew up in Bromley, Kent, not far from where I live now. I enjoyed many of his books as a child, but was particularly fascinated by this tale of Earth being invaded by evil aliens from Mars with their amazing machines.

The film Luke and his grandfather refer to on page 18 does exist. It was made in the USA in 1954 (the year I was born!). Although very different, it *is* based on H. G. Wells's novel, and also features aliens invading Earth with fantastic machines. Not surprisingly, it is one of my favourite movies!

1
The Disappearing Brother

'OK, Kelly,' said Dad with that sigh I'd heard before. 'Where is he, then? I distinctly remember asking you *not* to let him out of your sight while I went to get the tickets.'

We were standing in the middle of the huge, noisy, echoing station. It was full of people bustling about, but none of them was my brother. He had disappeared. Again.

It was something he had a habit of doing.

'I don't know, Dad,' I said. I crossed my fingers behind my back. 'I only turned round for a second. I would have looked for him, but I thought I'd better wait for you.'

I wasn't being totally honest, of course. My lovely brother and I had begun arguing the instant Dad had walked off. Luke had wanted to go exploring, and I'd said he wasn't allowed to.

But he'd gone anyway.

'That boy certainly picks his moments,' said

7

Dad, crossly. 'If he doesn't come back soon, you'll miss your train. And I don't think there's another one until tomorrow.'

'Does that mean we won't be able to stay with Gran and Grandad?' I said, trying not to sound too hopeful. I felt slightly ashamed about not wanting to go.

Don't get me wrong. I love my grandparents, I really do, and I like seeing them. The problem is that they live in the most boring place on the entire planet.

It's a small village, miles from anywhere. Staying there for a week every summer holidays was fine when Luke and I were little. But now it just isn't exciting enough.

There's no McDonald's, no cinema, no swimming-pool, and no other kids to hang out with. Not unless you count the odd baby or toddler. There isn't even a library.

'*Oh* no,' said Dad, shaking his head. 'It doesn't. You're going, even if I have to drive you myself. Your mother and I are looking forward to a week's peace and quiet.'

'Charming,' I said. 'Meanwhile, *I'll* be dying of boredom.'

'Don't exaggerate, Kelly,' said Dad. 'It won't be that bad. Besides, I've got a job for you.'

'What is it?' I said, suspiciously. I should have known what was coming next.

'I want you to make sure Luke doesn't get into any mischief this week,' he said. 'You know what he's like.'

I certainly do. Mum says 'curiosity' is Luke's middle name. If she means he's nosy, then I agree. Once Luke gets interested in something, he can't rest until he's found out all about it.

The trouble is that he never thinks of danger. He's the sort of person who sticks his finger into a hole to see what's inside, and is surprised when it gets bitten off.

I'm not like that. I'm much more careful, which is why I've always been lumbered with looking out for my brother. But I decided then and there I wasn't going to do it any longer.

'No way, Dad,' I said. 'Besides, you're only asking me because I'm the girl and he's the boy. It's sexist.'

'Now you know that's not true,' said Dad, indignantly. 'It's got more to do with you being the oldest . . . '

'Only by eighteen months,' I muttered.

' . . . *and* the most sensible,' he continued, ignoring me. 'Please, Kelly. I'm relying on you.'

'It's not fair,' I said. 'I'm fed up with being sensible. Luke is big enough to take care of himself.'

'Yeah, too right,' said a voice. 'And why are you talking about me, anyway? Have I missed anything interesting?'

Luke had come up behind us. There he

stood, happily chewing gum. He blew a bubble, popped it, and grinned. He was wearing that awful 'Beware – Alien Monster!' T-shirt of his.

He's fair-haired, and tall for his age. People say we look a lot alike, but I don't believe it.

I *won't* believe it.

'Where on *Earth* have you been?' said Dad. 'Your sister and I were beginning to get worried.'

Speak for yourself, Father, I thought. But I didn't say anything. I knew it wasn't worth it. Dad likes to think Luke and I are close, despite the arguments.

Sometimes I think parents live in a different world from children. At least mine do.

'All over,' said Luke, eagerly. 'Did you know there's something wrong with the departures board? I talked to a man who was fixing it, but he told me to clear off, so I . . . '

'OK, OK, I get the picture,' said Dad, holding up his hands. He looked annoyed. 'But that *is* awkward. How are we supposed to tell which platform your train leaves from?'

'That's easy,' said Luke. 'It's platform eight. I asked at the information desk. They gave me a

timetable, and some leaflets, too. There was one I wanted to show you . . . '

'Not just now, Luke,' sighed Dad. 'I think we ought to hurry up. I'm a bit worried about the car getting clamped . . . Here, Kelly, you'd better have the tickets.'

A few minutes later Luke and I were stowing our backpacks on the luggage rack of the only carriage with two free seats. We were going to have to sit next to each other, worse luck.

'Right, kids, cheerio,' said Dad at last. He gave us both a kiss. 'Grandad will be waiting for you at the other end. And what is it you've got to remember?'

'To behave ourselves,' Luke and I droned together.

Dad smiled, and got off. He stood waving on the platform as the train slowly eased out into the afternoon sunshine. I watched the houses and gardens begin to accelerate past.

After a while I opened one of the books I'd brought with me and started reading. I had plenty more. I was pretty sure I'd need something to keep me occupied at Gran and Grandad's.

But then I had no idea how busy I was going to be.

Or how terrified.

2
A Shooting Star

Have you ever wanted to murder somebody? Well, that's how *I* felt after we'd been on the train for a while. There are no prizes for guessing who my intended victim was, either.

As soon as we left the station, Luke started playing with the hand-held computer game he takes *everywhere*. He sat there like some kind of robot, completely absorbed in the tiny screen.

At first I stuck to my book, and tried to ignore him. But it's hard to concentrate when the person next to you keeps bleeping. He didn't even notice when we arrived.

I had to kick him twice before he realized where we were.

'Hello, kids,' said Grandad. He was waiting for us on the platform. 'Did you have a good journey?'

'No, Luke spoiled it,' I said, as we followed Grandad into the car park. 'He was irritating the whole time.'

'I was not,' snapped Luke. 'Anyway, you're only jealous because you haven't got a Game Zapper like me.'

'That's where you're wrong, smarty-pants,' I said. 'I think those things are *stupid*.'

'Fat lot *you* know,' said Luke. 'You couldn't even . . .'

'Bong! End of round one!' said Grandad, laughing. We waited by the car while he unlocked the doors. 'And thanks very much, you two. I knew you wouldn't let me down.'

Luke and I glanced at each other. Luke shrugged. He obviously didn't know what Grandad was talking about either.

'I don't understand, Grandad,' I said.

'What a pair you are,' he said, smiling and shaking his head. 'I bet your Gran a pound you'd have your first argument before we got back to the house. And I was right, wasn't I?'

'That wasn't a proper argument, Grandad,' said Luke, grinning. 'You should hear us when we *really* get going.'

'I'm sure I will,' said Grandad. 'But I'd rather wait until we're at home, if it's all the same to you. Your Gran must be wondering

where we are. I'll just put those in the boot . . . '

Grandad took our backpacks, and soon we were on our way out of town. The journey wasn't over yet. We still had the worst part ahead of us, the long drive to the village.

There's only one road, which means the place is isolated and easily cut off. It happened last winter in the snow. I'm just glad *I* wasn't staying at the time.

The sun had gone down by the time we turned the corner into the High Street. But even though it was dark, I could tell that nothing much had changed. It never does.

There were the same old houses, the same old pub, the same old bus stop, and probably the same old man being taken for a walk past Mr Clarke's mini-market by the same old dog.

Mr Clarke waved, and we waved back. As always, his fat, ancient ginger cat was curled up in the window. It opened its green eyes for a second, then went back to sleep.

I yawned. I could feel myself getting bored already.

'Tired, love?' said Grandad as we went past the church. The house was on the edge of the village. 'Not far now. Once you've eaten you can have a bath and go to bed.'

'Do we have to?' asked Luke. 'I wanted to watch *The War of the Worlds* on TV tonight. I've seen it before, but it's great.'

'Here we are,' said Grandad, turning into the drive. 'Is that the one where the aliens nearly take over the world, but they die at the end because they catch 'flu, or something?'

Luke said that was right, they couldn't resist Earth viruses and bugs. Then I spotted Gran in the doorway. Grandad stopped the car. Luke and I got out and ran over to give Gran a hug.

'I can't believe the size of you!' she said, kissing us. 'What have your Mum and Dad been feeding you on? You're both about three times bigger than you were when I saw you last.'

'I'll tell you one thing that hasn't changed, though,' said Grandad, taking our backpacks out of the boot. 'They still argue just as much. Which means you owe me . . . '

'Hey, what's *that*?' said Luke suddenly, pointing upwards.

We looked and saw . . . well, I found out

what it was later. But at that moment we all thought the bright, moving spot of light in the night sky was nothing more than a shooting star.

'Well, I never . . . ' said Grandad as it disappeared. 'Do you know, I saw one exactly like that yesterday. I reckon it was about the same time in the evening, too.'

'That's right, I remember you telling me,' said Gran. 'We must be due for a lot of luck. Quickly, kids! You're supposed to make a wish when you see a shooting star.'

I don't think Luke did. He just went on and on about meteors burning up in the atmosphere. But I closed my eyes, and wished that something exciting would happen during our stay.

I should have wished for something else.

Grandad put the car in the garage, and we went indoors. Soon Gran was calling us to the dining-room. I hadn't realized how hungry I felt. And I'd forgotten what a good cook Gran was.

'I'll ring your Mum and Dad,' said Grandad, going into the hall. 'They'll want to know you've arrived safely.' We heard him pick up the phone. 'Strange,' he said. 'The line's dead.'

'Are you sure?' said Gran.

It was true. Grandad said there must be a fault, and that he'd have to go into the village in the morning to report it to the engineers. He said he'd call Mum and Dad then.

The television chose that very same evening

to break down, too. We couldn't get anything on it but interference. So we had an early night after all, much to Luke's disappointment.

Our week's stay wasn't starting too wonderfully. Oh well, I thought, as I got into bed. At least I don't have to share a room with Luke like I did when I was younger.

'Night-night, love,' said Gran, closing the door. 'I'll see you in the morning.'

She couldn't have been more wrong.

3
Strange Awakening

When I woke up the next day, I lay for a while in my warm bed, staring at the ceiling. Eventually I turned to look at the small clock Gran had left on the bedside cabinet.

It was nearly quarter past nine.

That was odd, I thought. Grandad didn't usually let us have a lie-in when we stayed. He was always up early, and called us long before eight, let alone this late.

I got out of bed and put on my dressing-gown. I wondered if Grandad had decided I deserved some extra rest. Even though I'd hated to admit it, I *had* been very tired last night.

I'd certainly slept heavily, anyway. For once I couldn't remember having a single dream, and I still felt a little slow and dozy. I had a bit of a headache, too.

My appetite was definitely all right, though. My tummy was rumbling, and I was looking forward to one of Gran's terrific breakfasts. So off I went downstairs.

I noticed that the house was very quiet. I couldn't hear the radio from the kitchen, which was unusual. Gran and Grandad always liked listening to the news in the mornings.

I paused in the hall. The front door was open, and the rug was in a sort of heap on the doorstep. Now that *was* peculiar, I thought. Gran was an incredibly tidy person.

Why would she have left the door open and the rug like that?

Maybe it's part of some big cleaning operation, I said to myself. Dad reckons his mum is the only person he's ever heard of who does spring-cleaning all year round.

She was probably going to shake the dust off it outside, or something. She's a real fresh-air fiend as well, is our Gran. That's why she lives in the country, I suppose.

I shrugged and headed for the kitchen, a smile ready to greet Gran and Grandad. But my smile soon faded. There was no one in there, and no wonderful breakfast waiting for me.

There were some dirty pots on the draining

board from dinner the evening before. The
dishwasher was only half-filled. And a tea-
towel was lying on the floor by the swing-bin.

I was beginning to feel uneasy.

This isn't right, I thought. This isn't the way
it should be. I went over to the window and
looked out. I was hoping Gran and Grandad
would be in the garden. But they weren't.

I left the kitchen and went into the front
room. They weren't in there, and neither were
they in any of the other downstairs rooms. I
stood in the hall and called out.

'Gran!' I shouted. 'Grandad! Where *are* you?'

My words were like pebbles dropped into a dark pool. I waited and waited, but there was no answer.

The silence lapped softly back into place around me.

I know, I thought with relief. I'll bet they've just over-slept. It wasn't something I'd ever known them do, but perhaps you needed more sleep when you got old. That *must* be it.

I ran upstairs and along the landing to their bedroom door. It was shut, so I gripped the handle and turned it. I opened the door slowly, and peeked in, certain I would find them.

But they weren't there.

The bed was made, almost as if it hadn't been slept in.

I leant against the door-frame and tried not to panic. I remember telling myself there had to be some sort of logical explanation for Gran and Grandad to go missing.

Then a hand grabbed my shoulder, and my heart nearly jumped out of my mouth. I whirled round and saw . . . Luke.

'Surprise, surprise!' he said, and laughed at

me. I could tell by the sleep in his eyes that he had only just got up. He was still in his pyjamas and dressing-gown, too.

'That wasn't funny, Luke,' I snapped. I was very cross.

'I thought it was,' he said. 'Why were you creeping about, anyway? And why didn't Grandad wake me up like he usually does? Sleeping late's given me a headache . . . What's going on?'

'I haven't got a clue,' I said. I explained that Gran and Grandad seemed to have vanished into thin air.

'Don't be daft,' said Luke. 'They're bound to be *somewhere*. They wouldn't just go off and leave us. I mean, they're not allowed to, are they? It's against the law, isn't it?'

'All right then, clever-clogs,' I said, wanting to believe him, but also not wanting to admit he might know better than me. 'If you're so brilliant, *you* find them.'

'OK, I will,' he said cockily, and went downstairs.

But within ten minutes, Luke was as puzzled as me. Gran and Grandad were definitely not in the house. They weren't in the garden shed, either. And the car was still in the garage.

We were completely alone.

'Well, I don't know about you,' I said, 'but I'm going to get washed and dressed. And then I intend to walk into the village and ask Mr Clarke if he knows where they are.'

'Why don't we phone him?' Luke said.

'Because the phone's still not working, dumbo,' I said as I went upstairs. 'I tried it again.'

'Oh, right,' said Luke. There was a pause, and then I heard his feet on the stairs behind me. 'I'll come too.'

I was glad he'd said that. Not that I told him, though.

When I was ready, I went back downstairs to the kitchen. My tummy wouldn't have let me go out unless I ate something. Luke decided he wanted breakfast as well, so we had some cereal.

'This milk isn't very cold,' Luke muttered when he got it out of the fridge. But I didn't take any notice.

The sun was shining when we set off down the drive, and my headache had gone. We turned left out of the gate and started along the road towards the village. It was ten o'clock.

We went past the church, then stopped. We stood looking at the High Street we had come through the night before.

What I saw sent a chill creeping up my spine.

4
The Empty Village

There seemed to have been an accident about fifty metres ahead of us, just beyond the pub. A car had crashed into a lamp-post and was partly blocking the road.

'Wow! Do you think anyone's been hurt?' said Luke. 'We'd better go and see if we can help!'

'Luke, *stop*!' I shouted. 'You don't know, it might be dangerous . . . '

But it was too late. Luke's nosiness had already sent him haring off towards the car. I followed as quickly as I could. When I caught up, he was peering through the rear window.

I hung back. I didn't want to catch sight of anything gory, although I needn't have worried. The windscreen was cracked and one of the doors was open, but the car was empty.

'Maybe we just missed the crash last night,' said Luke. 'If the driver was injured they probably took him to the hospital in town. There isn't much damage, though.'

'*She* might have been a woman,' I said. I get annoyed when he just assumes that boys and men do absolutely everything in this world. 'You didn't think of that, did you?'

'Sorry I spoke,' said Luke. Then he paused. I could almost hear the cogs grinding as he thought. 'Mind you, there's something funny about this,' he said, at last.

'What do you mean?' I asked, my own sense of uneasiness deepening with every word he spoke.

'Usually the police tow cars away pretty quickly after an accident,' he said. 'But it's still here. They haven't even put out any warning signs in the road.'

'Perhaps they haven't had time yet,' I said.

'It's one of the first things they do, stupid,' he said. 'Especially when the road is blocked like this. Otherwise every car that comes round the corner might hit the wreck.'

'So why haven't they done it then, Mr Expert?' I said.

'I don't know, do I?' he replied, grumpily. 'And where *is* everybody, anyway? This has to be the most interesting thing that's happened here for centuries, and the place is deserted.'

It was a question that had been nagging at me ever since we'd entered the village. So far we hadn't seen a soul, and it was very quiet. In fact, it was definitely *too* quiet.

There were no faces in any of the windows, nobody was waiting at the bus stop, and none of the elderly villagers were out being taken for a walk by their dogs.

I couldn't even hear any birds singing.

'Come on,' I said, edging round the crashed car so that I could keep to the pavement. 'Let's go and talk to Mr Clarke. I just want to find out where Gran and Grandad are.'

'Wait for me,' said Luke, scurrying in my footsteps.

Mr Clarke's mini-market was only a few metres further along. But before I reached it I could see something was wrong. A trail of white powder led out of the door and into the road.

I bent down and saw that it was sugar. It crunched under my trainers as I went in. The interior of the shop was darker than outside, and it took several seconds for my eyes to adjust.

When they did, a fist of fear tightened in my chest.

I didn't have to go any further to see that the

mini-market had been ransacked. Some of the shelves had been cleared, and a pile of packets, tins, and bottles lay on the floor.

There was no sign of Mr Clarke.

'What's up?' asked Luke, pushing past me. He stopped just inside the doorway and looked around. His jaw dropped. 'Incredible!' he said. 'Mr Clarke's had a burglary!'

To begin with I thought he was right. But I soon changed my mind. From where I was standing I could see the cash till was open, and there was still plenty of money in it.

There was something else I spotted, though. Something so strange it made the hairs stand up on the back of my neck.

'Luke, look,' I said, peering at a gooey red line running down the label on a jar of strawberry jam. 'Somebody's made a hole in this . . . there are holes in *everything*!'

I'd never heard of a burglar who did *that*.

We couldn't understand it. Each container, whether it was cardboard, metal or glass, had an identical hole. The insides had oozed or trickled out to make an awful mess.

'Now this is what I call *seriously* weird,' said Luke, picking his way over to the freezer cabinet. 'Hey, it's all melting in here! It looks like the electricity's been turned off, too.'

'That's *it*,' I said. I felt myself on the verge of losing control. 'I've had enough. I'm going to find someone who can tell me what this is about – if it's the last thing I do!'

I marched outside and into the middle of the road. I shouted for ages, hoping that someone, anyone, would reply. But nobody did. The village seemed to be completely empty.

'Have you noticed most of the doors are open?' said Luke, softly. I hadn't, but now I saw that they were. 'It's almost as if everyone left in a hurry last night . . . '

'But why, Luke?' I said. 'And where have they gone?'

'I've got it!' he said, sounding excited. 'Maybe a nuclear power station has blown up, and the whole village has been evacuated because of the radiation!'

'Don't be ridiculous,' I said, angrily. 'Gran

and Grandad would never have left us behind if that had happened, and you know it. There must be some other explanation.'

Luke wouldn't have it, though. He was convinced he'd come up with the answer, so we stood there in the middle of the eerie, abandoned village, arguing at the tops of our voices.

'Shut up a minute, will you?' said Luke suddenly. 'I think I heard something. There it is again . . .'

I could hear it as well now, a strange sort of rustling noise that was getting closer, and closer, and closer. Luke and I turned together . . . and saw what was making it.

I stood rooted to the spot, too stunned to speak.

5
The Mystery Monster

I was staring at the most incredible thing I had ever encountered, an object so strange I thought I must have been dreaming. No, that's wrong. I *hoped* I was dreaming.

I didn't want it to be real.

It was about as long as a car, but much lower, and looked like a giant, oval plate that had been turned upside down. It was covered in green and black zig-zag stripes, too.

As it moved, I saw that it seemed to be floating on a shimmering silver wave. It didn't take long to figure out that the wave was almost certainly the source of the rustling sound.

Then something more ominous dawned on me. It wasn't moving quickly, but it *was* heading in a very definite direction – ours. I gulped. That made me feel very uncomfortable indeed.

'Luke, I don't like this,' I whispered, grabbing his arm. 'Come on, let's get out of here.'

He didn't budge, so I looked at his face. My heart sank. I had seen those wide eyes and that vacant grin many times before. They always had a very simple meaning.

Luke had fallen in love.

'Amazing,' he said. 'What do you think it could be?'

'I don't know,' I said. 'And I don't . . . '

I was going to say I didn't care, but I never got to finish my sentence. The rustling had stopped, and the mystery monster had halted about ten metres away from us.

I watched, horrified, as a small opening appeared near the front. A new noise began, an ear-splitting, high-pitched whining, and a thin, grey rod gradually emerged.

Even from that distance I could tell it was wickedly sharp.

There was a click, the whining stopped, and the rustling started again. The monster was moving forward once more. Only now I thought it was aiming something deadly at us.

I wanted to run. But Luke had other ideas.

'It's fantastic,' he said. 'I *must* have a closer look.'

'Don't be crazy, Luke,' I said, trying desperately to hold him back. From the corner of my
eye I could see the thing was almost on top of
us. 'I won't let you!'

But Luke pulled free of my grasp, and I lost
my balance. I fell down, directly in the
monster's path. The rustling grew louder and
louder until it filled my head, and that sharp,
menacing rod loomed above me . . .

I flung an arm over my face. I heard that
high-pitched whining once more, and I felt

something jolt hard into the ground just beyond my shoulder. But that was all.

I was alive. I could barely believe it.

I carefully lowered my arm and saw a quivering wall of silver centimetres from the tip of my nose. I rolled over and scrambled away as fast as I could.

'That was close,' said Luke, not that he sounded particularly bothered. He did help me to my feet, though. 'It looked like you'd really had it there for a minute. Mind you . . . '

I didn't stop to listen. There was only one thought in my mind – escape. But this time it was Luke who grabbed me. He gripped my T-shirt and wouldn't let go.

'Please, Kelly, wait,' he said, real pleading in his voice. 'And just *look*, will you? There's nothing to be afraid of, honest . . . I don't think it wants to hurt anyone.'

I stopped struggling for a second and glanced over his shoulder. The thing was still sitting there on its silver wave, but now it was doing something even more bizarre.

That sharp point had penetrated the pavement. As I watched, the rod started spinning, slowly at first, but then faster and faster. The whining noise changed to a deep hum.

Next, a light appeared inside the rod, then another, and another. Finally they formed a continuous stream that came from the ground and went into the main body of the monster.

It seemed to be sucking something out of the Earth.

'Oh yeah?' I said. 'So why did it try to kill me?'

'It didn't,' said Luke. 'You were just in the

way. Can't you see that? It probably doesn't even know we're here.'

'What are you talking about, Luke?' I said, keeping a wary eye on the thing. I was ready to run if it made a move.

'Use your brain, Kelly,' he sighed in that irritating, superior way of his. 'It's a *machine*.'

I realized that made sense as soon as he said it. Now I was able to think more calmly, there *was* something very machine-like in the way the thing had behaved.

'Maybe it is,' I said, reluctantly. 'But if that makes you feel any safer, you're mad. I've never seen anything like it in my life. And don't tell me *you* have, either.'

'No, I haven't,' he said, going over to it. 'But that doesn't mean much. It might be top secret. There's all sorts of stuff we don't know about, especially things to do with radiation . . . '

Luke was obviously still convinced the village was empty because it had been evacuated. I was beginning to think he might be right. But why hadn't we been woken up and taken too?

Was it, I wondered, because something bad

42

had happened to Gran and Grandad? Suddenly I couldn't stop horrible pictures of them in pain crowding into my mind.

But why hadn't the same happened to us? If there was deadly radiation everywhere, why hadn't *we* been affected? How come we were still walking around, fit and healthy?

An awful thought occurred to me.

Perhaps for some reason it took longer with children. I might start feeling ill at any second. Luke and I could collapse, and no one would be there to help us. We might even die.

I shuddered. This was like a nightmare. I wanted to pinch myself and wake up and find everything *normal* . . . I couldn't understand how Luke was managing to stay so calm.

Then he called out my name, and I knew he wasn't any more.

'Kelly!' he yelled. 'Quick, over here . . . '

6
The Black Globe

Luke was standing by the mystery monster, but it was no longer the centre of his attention. His gaze was now fixed firmly on something he had seen further down the High Street.

'What is it, Luke?' I said when I was beside him.

He didn't answer, so I turned to look in the same direction. I spotted what he was staring at immediately. I closed my eyes, hoping it would go away. But when I opened them, it hadn't.

A black globe was coming towards us. It was roughly the size of a beach ball, and was moving quite slowly. Oh yes, and there was one other thing I couldn't help noticing.

It was flying.

There were no visible engines or propellers, and unlike the other machine, it made no sound. Because of that, it seemed much more . . . well, *evil* is the only way I can describe it.

It stopped about a metre in front of us, and

hovered on a level with our faces. One second, two seconds, three seconds, four seconds went by. Each of them an eternity.

Then the globe started moving back. It went slowly at first, picked up speed, flashed down the High Street, rose up, flew over the roofs . . . and disappeared from sight.

I let out my breath. I realized I'd been holding it from the instant I'd seen the globe.

'OK, Luke,' I said. 'Let me hear you try explaining *that*.'

'Well, I, er . . . I can't,' he mumbled, scratching his head. For once he had run out of words. But it didn't last. 'It was pretty good though, wasn't it?' he said, and smiled.

'Oh, Luke,' I said crossly. 'Can't you be serious for once? We might be in danger! And what about Gran and Grandad? We don't even know where they are. Or had that slipped your mind?'

'As a matter of fact, it hadn't,' snapped Luke, defensively. 'I was going to say we should try and . . . '

He was interrupted by a loud buzzing noise. I whipped round, and saw a small, dark shape shoot out of an open door. I jumped backwards, thinking it might be a rat. But it wasn't.

'Gangway!' shouted Luke, rushing after it. He pounced, and let out a whoop of triumph. 'There, now what do you think of *this*?' he said, showing me what was cupped in his hands.

It was a machine, identical in everything but size to the big one that had nearly run me over, right down to the green and black zig-zag stripes. It even had its own little silver wave.

'Not a lot,' I replied, although to be truthful I was actually beginning to get interested myself. 'It reminds me of an insect. It's like some kind of extra-large cockroach.'

'Yeah, that's what I thought,' said Luke. 'But as soon as I picked it up I realized it was more like a centipede, or even a millipede. Check *these* out. I'm glad I'm not ticklish.'

He flipped the machine over to show me its underneath. Suddenly I saw the silver wave wasn't solid. It was actually made of hundreds of fast-moving, tiny, shiny *legs*.

I turned to look at the big machine. It was still in the same place, the grey rod pulsing with lights. Now I could see that *its* silver wave was really a collection of legs, too.

Then I heard a click, and turned back to discover that the pocket–sized version also had a rod, but one so titchy it was like a pin. Luke was watching, fascinated, as it slowly emerged.

'Be careful, Luke . . . ' I said.

'Stop fussing, Kelly,' he said. 'You always
... OWW!'

The pin had jabbed into Luke's hand. He
dropped the tiny machine as if he'd been stung.
It landed on the pavement and sped away,
buzzing more loudly than ever.

'I told you so,' I said. 'Maybe next time
you'll listen.'

'Oh, shut up,' said Luke, rubbing at his
palm. 'I'll bet it didn't mean any harm. It was
worth it, anyway. I might never get another
chance to look at one of those things again.'

Somehow I had a feeling he would. And I was right. Within minutes a third machine had come buzzing out of a different door, then another, and another, and another . . .

We saw dozens of machines over the next half-hour or so. Some were small, some were medium-sized, and a couple more were almost as big as the first one we had met.

And they were all built to the same basic plan.

The village was full of them. They went in and out of houses, criss-crossed the High Street, crawled along walls. They didn't bump into each other, and took no notice of Luke or me.

The black globe did, though, I was sure. I caught sight of it hovering nearby on several occasions, and I got the distinct impression it was keeping an eye on us.

The thought made me go cold all over.

'Luke, that black globe thing . . . ' I whispered. 'Don't look now, but it's come back, and I think it's following us.'

'What?' he said. 'Where is it? There's nothing there . . . '

'It's gone, you twit,' I said. 'You scared it off.'

'Oh well, never mind about that,' he said, eagerly. 'I've just worked out what these machines are. It's obvious, really.'

'Not to me,' I said, trying to see where the globe had gone.

'They're probes,' he said, sounding very pleased with himself. 'They're testing everything for radiation . . . It's what the rods are for. That's why they poke into things.'

I knew instantly he'd hit the nail on the head.

It explained so much . . . the way the machines bustled around, each one knowing exactly where it was going, and the holes in all those packets, tins and bottles.

'And that means someone must be controlling them!' I said. 'Come on, Luke . . . they're probably outside the village, on the road. Gran and Grandad will be there too, I'm sure of it!'

I started running down the High Street. For the first time in my life I didn't even think about being careful.

But as I went careering round the corner, I realized that perhaps I should have done . . .

7
Separate Ways

I skidded to a stop, and Luke ran into me. I turned, took his arm, and dived behind the cover of a bush to our left. I shoved him down and practically sat on top of him.

'Hey!' he said, crossly. 'What's the big idea?'

'Sssh!' I hissed at him like a demented snake. 'Just keep your mouth shut while I think of how to save us!'

'Save us from *what*?' he said, trying to push me off.

I didn't say anything. Instead, I just pointed.

'Wow!' he said, peering through the leaves. He was so surprised I thought for a second his eyes were going to pop out on stalks, like a cartoon character's. 'That's totally *mega*!'

I couldn't have put it better myself. Less than a hundred metres away something enormous was blocking the only road that left the village. Something that almost made my mind reel.

We had found the biggest machine of all.

Luke and I hadn't seen it from the High Street because it wasn't as tall as the houses, although it was pretty long. It certainly wouldn't have fitted into our school playground.

One glance told me it was related to the other machines. It was the same general shape, and was covered in the same pattern of green and black stripes. But there were some differences.

It wasn't sitting on a silver wave, for a start. It had legs, but these were squat and powerful-looking, and there couldn't have been more than eight or ten of them on each side.

And it didn't have a rod, either. Instead, there was a broad, dark opening in the front. A yellow strip hung out of it. This ran along the road for some distance towards the village.

I shivered, even though the sun was warm on my back. The whole scene made me think of a giant insect with its tongue out, waiting to snap up some unsuspecting prey . . .

Suddenly I noticed Luke wasn't looking at it any more. He was lying on his back in the small space behind the bush. His eyes were shut tight, and his fists clenched by his sides.

Then he began drumming his heels on the ground and making peculiar noises. I listened, and he seemed to be saying 'Yes . . . *yes* . . . ' and moaning softly to himself.

'Luke!' I whispered. I was frightened. I was convinced the radiation had finally got to him, and that I would be the next victim. 'Luke, speak to me . . . are you all right?'

'I'm fine,' he said, opening his eyes and sitting up. He grinned. 'I feel terrific, and this is the best day of my life. Cheer up, Kelly. We're going to be famous!'

'What *are* you talking about now, Luke?' I said.

I realized he hadn't been having a fit. In fact, I should have spotted it was put on. Don't ask me why, but it's Luke's usual way of showing he's absolutely ecstatic about something.

'Can't you see?' he said, much too loudly for my liking. 'We're going to be the first people to make contact with creatures from another world, with aliens. *That's a spaceship.*'

'Keep your voice down!' I hissed. 'How can you be sure? You said yourself there must be all kinds of top secret stuff. I'll bet it's from another country, not another planet.'

'Yeah, but then you probably still believe in Santa Claus and the Tooth Fairy, don't you?' said Luke. 'Come *on*, Kelly. For heaven's sake, just look at it. What else *could* it be?'

'What about all the machines, then?' I said.

'They must be robots, or something,' said Luke.

'All right, so maybe it is a . . . a spaceship,' I whispered. It was amazing, I thought, but it did explain a lot. Especially the black globe. 'That only makes things worse.'

'Don't be such a wimp,' he said. 'This could be our big . . . '

'Quiet!' I said.

Luke looked daggers at me, but did what he was told.

I had heard the unmistakable sound of rustling that meant another machine was approaching. I parted the leaves, and saw a medium-sized one moving quite quickly towards the spaceship.

I watched it slide up the yellow strip and disappear inside. Something colourful seemed to be tangled in its legs at the rear. It could have been a piece of cloth, or a towel.

Or maybe even the kind of rug you'd have in a hall.

'Is it OK for me to speak now, miss?' said Luke, irritably. I'd been thinking so deeply I'd almost forgotten he was there.

'Did you see that?' I said. 'There was something caught . . . '

'Belt up a minute, will you?' he said. I turned to face him. 'Now, would you mind getting out of my way, please? I've got an appointment with some aliens.'

'Oh, no, you haven't,' I said, not moving. 'If you think I'm dozy enough to let you go any-where near that . . . that spaceship, then you've got another thing coming.'

'Try and stop me,' he said, a stubborn look on his face. 'I'm fed up with you treating me like a baby and bossing me around all the time. You're worse than Mum and Dad.'

'Please, Luke,' I said. 'Be sensible, will you?'

'As far as I'm concerned, I *am* being sensible,' he said. 'I reckon that whoever's in there is friendly. And I'm only going to say hello. So tell me, what's wrong with that?'

'Er, all sorts of things,' I said, although I couldn't think of any just then. 'Anyway, Dad said that as I'm the oldest . . . '

'I'm not listening any more,' said Luke, angrily. 'And I'm not missing out on this just because you're a scaredy-cat. But then that's what *all* girls are, isn't it?' he sneered.

That was the last straw.

'OK, do what you want,' I said, standing up. I was furious. 'But don't come running to *me* when you get in trouble.'

'Don't worry, I *won't*,' he said, dodging past.

I watched him stroll jauntily along the road towards the yellow strip. He was whistling, and that stupid Game Zapper thing was sticking out of the back pocket of his jeans.

Then I turned and walked away.

8
Kelly's Choice

I went straight along the High Street, which was still as busy as ever with buzzing and rustling machines. I felt so angry, I just couldn't *believe* how idiotic my little brother was being.

But that was his problem, I thought as I marched past the church. It certainly had nothing to do with me. My days of looking out for him were finished for ever.

I strode up the drive towards Gran and Grandad's house, fuming inside. I stopped at the front door . . . then realized I had made a big mistake myself earlier that morning.

I had forgotten to take a key.

I had carefully shut the door behind us when we'd left, and I hadn't given a single thought to getting in again. Now I couldn't believe how stupid *I* had been.

I stood chewing on a fingernail. I was stumped. Part of me wanted to bang on the door and scream out for Gran and Grandad, hoping that by some miracle they had returned.

But I knew they hadn't. The house was silent, the windows staring like a blind man's sightless eyes. I flipped open the letterbox and looked through. No one was there.

The hall rug was where it should be, though. I'd brought it in before we'd set out. It reminded me of the machine I'd seen entering the spaceship, the one with something caught in its legs.

What if Gran and Grandad's hall rug had got tangled up in the same way, and been dragged on to the front doorstep? That would certainly explain how it had ended up there in a heap.

But it also meant one of the machines must have come into the house during the night, while Luke and I had been asleep. Why hadn't we heard it, though? And how had it got in?

I couldn't imagine it knocking politely, or slowly extending its probing rod to ring the bell. It definitely didn't have a key. Maybe it had used the back door . . . *The back door*!

I ran to the side gate, which wasn't locked, thank goodness. I went round to the rear of the

house. The back door *was* locked, but I knew where Gran and Grandad hid a spare key.

It was in the garage, underneath the bottom tray in Grandad's tool-box. Grandad had shown it to me last time Luke and I had visited. 'Just in case you ever need it,' he'd said.

I didn't have any trouble getting into the garage, either. Grandad never locked the door that let you in from the garden. I pushed it open. The cool darkness smelt of oil and dust.

I lifted the tool-box lid. I hardly dared to look, but there it was, a thin, silver shape nestling among several heavy spanners. I took it out, and returned to the house.

I unlocked the back door, went in, and closed it gently behind me. The kitchen was as I'd seen it last, except for one change. A puddle was spreading round the foot of the fridge.

I remembered what Luke had said about the milk not being very cold, and the food melting in the fridge at Mr Clarke's mini-market. It seemed that the same was happening here.

I tried the switch on the wall, but the lights didn't come on. I checked the taps, and they were still running, so I got myself a glass of water. I was very thirsty.

Then I sat down at the table to think.

My brain felt as if it was on overload. I wanted to try and make sense of what I'd seen, but I had no idea where to begin. The whole world seemed to have gone crazy overnight.

I went through yesterday's events in my mind. I was looking for some clues. The train journey, being picked up by Grandad, seeing that shooting star when we arrived . . .

The shooting star!

It had to be the answer! The strange stuff had started *after* we'd seen it. I realized now that the shooting star and the spaceship must have been one and the same thing.

That was where the interference on the television had come from, I was sure. And it probably had a lot to do with the phone not working. Of course, I thought . . .

I couldn't understand why I hadn't seen it immediately. We had been sealed off from the outside. We couldn't receive any news, and we couldn't get in touch with anyone.

It was all very sinister. If I was right, Luke had been completely wrong about radiation and everyone being evacuated. *Nobody knew what was going on here.*

So where were Gran and Grandad and the other people? Maybe they had never left, I thought. Maybe the truth was that they'd been captured and taken on board the spaceship . . .

Luke and I might simply have been over-looked.

It made terrifying sense. I didn't know why aliens might want to kidnap a large number of human beings. But I'd seen enough science fiction films to make me very, very worried.

Pictures of Gran and Grandad surrounded by hideous creatures from outer space crept into my mind. Then they were blotted out by an image of Luke strolling towards that yellow strip.

In my memory it looked even more like a

huge tongue. I stood up. Suddenly I felt very, very guilty. Because I'd lost my temper, I had let my brother walk into appalling danger.

I should never have allowed it. I should have done *anything* to stop him. What would I say to Mum and Dad if I got out of this and Luke didn't? I *had* to save him, and the others.

It seemed to me I faced a choice between two alternatives. I could find a way out of the village and go for help. But the risk was that even if I made it, I might be too late.

Or I could try and do something myself,

although the thought of going into that space-ship made me feel sick with fear.

I swallowed hard. I had to make my mind up, and *fast*.

I did. I left the house, locked the back door, and headed for the garage. I put the key in Grandad's tool-box where I had found it. Then I took something else out.

One of Grandad's heavy spanners.

I thought it might come in handy as a weapon . . .

9
Into the Darkness

You probably think I had gone completely mad. I did have a moment of doubt myself as I turned out of Gran and Grandad's gate and headed towards the village once more.

What was I *doing*? I couldn't possibly take on whatever was in that spaceship and win. I slowed down and thought about making a break for it – in the opposite direction . . .

Then I pulled myself together. I'd made my choice, and I was going to stick to it. I might be the careful type, but I can also be pretty determined when I set my mind to something.

I wasn't going to stop being cautious, though. For some reason I had a feeling it was my only real hope. That proved to be right, although not in a way I could ever have imagined.

At the time, it meant I was already beginning to work out a plan. I had no intention of walking up to the spaceship and asking to be let

in, which was probably what Luke had done.

I had something different in mind. It didn't take a genius to realize I'd have a much better chance of success if I could somehow manage to sneak on board unnoticed.

The question was – how?

I racked my brains as I hurried along the High Street, avoiding machines. I couldn't be sure, but there seemed to be fewer than earlier. I didn't hang around to count them.

Ten minutes after leaving Gran and

Grandad's house, I was behind the bush where I'd argued with Luke. It was gone twelve o'clock, and my stomach was asking about the next meal.

I tried not to think about food. I peered through the leaves at the spaceship, which was squatting in the same place. That yellow strip still led into its dark interior.

I couldn't see Luke anywhere.

As I watched, several small machines shot out of the village and buzzed into the spaceship. A couple of medium-sized ones bustled along next, followed by lots more of the tiny sort.

I seem to have arrived at rush hour, I thought. Then it occurred to me that this would be my opportunity. All I needed was for a big machine to join the traffic jam.

And that's exactly what came rustling down the road, almost perfectly on cue. If anything, it was even bigger than the one that had nearly flattened me. That made it just right.

I dashed out from behind the cover of the bush and ran over to the machine. I bent down low and trotted close behind it. I reckoned that would make me more difficult to spot.

After a while, the rustling sound changed and became softer. I looked down and saw that we had reached the yellow strip. It was smooth and shiny, but my trainers didn't slip on it.

The entrance to the spaceship was fifty metres away, then forty, thirty . . . it was a black hole. I couldn't see anything inside. The machines seemed to disappear into the darkness.

From twenty metres out the yellow strip started to rise gradually. I could jump, I thought. I don't have to do this. Fifteen metres, ten metres, five . . . It was now or never.

Two heartbeats later I crossed the threshold.

You won't be surprised to hear I felt very scared. I expected to be grabbed by slimy alien tentacles at any second, and dragged off screaming . . . but it didn't happen.

It wasn't as dark as I'd thought it was going to be, either. In front of me was the entrance to an oval passageway, about two metres high, with a strange orange glow at its far end.

The machine and I were still moving along the yellow strip, which became the floor of the passageway. I hate enclosed spaces, so I hoped the passageway was short.

It was. Suddenly we emerged, but all I could see was an orange haze. It seemed to fill the air with a sort of throbbing that set my teeth on edge and made my head hurt.

I stood still and the machine rustled away. I shielded my eyes and squinted, trying to make out my surroundings. And gradually things started to become clearer.

I saw now that the yellow strip split the orange glow into two equal halves. It was like a road cutting through the middle of two great banks of neon lights.

Then I realized each of those lights contained something. I walked slowly over to the nearest one, and peered at the dark shape within. That's when my jaw dropped.

It was Mr Clarke.

He had one hand extended, and the other looked as if it was about to pick something up. But he was absolutely motionless. He was more like a wax dummy than a human being.

Next to him was a much smaller glow. I bent down, and found myself looking at a fat ginger cat. It was curled up, exactly as it had been when I'd seen it last, in Mr Clarke's window.

I walked a little further and there was someone else, a woman in a sitting position, with her arms held out. But she had no chair. The orange glow was holding her off the floor.

There were others, all trapped in orange light, all frozen somehow in mid-action. Then it clicked. Mr Clarke had opened his cash till, the woman had been driving a car that crashed . . .

The people of the village had been captured unawares and brought here. It was the spookiest thing I'd ever seen. They were like a collection of living statues.

At least, I *hoped* they were living.

And then I thought of Gran and Grandad. If everyone else was here, they must be, too. I soon found them. They were standing behind the vicar and his wife and children.

Grandad was stooping the way he always does over the dishwasher, and Gran looked as if she'd just dropped something. I remembered the tea-towel. Tears filled my eyes.

Seeing them there like that was just too much.

I didn't have time to do anything, though. I felt a prickling in the back of my neck. I turned round . . .

And saw the black globe heading straight for me.

10
Under Fire

I drew in a breath sharply as it came closer. I hadn't liked the evil thing from the moment I had first seen it. I liked it even less now it had sneaked up silently and caught me.

It was coming from the direction of the entrance, so there was no way back. I could only go further into the spaceship, and that, it seemed, was what the globe wanted me to do.

For this time it didn't stop. It just kept moving steadily, relentlessly, menacingly towards me. I started retreating, unable to take my eyes off it for a second.

I was glad I didn't. Suddenly an orange spot appeared on its surface. It grew, and grew, then leapt out and changed into an orange circle as big as a bike wheel.

It spun through the air until it was crackling a metre directly above me. Then it began to descend, making my head ache so much I thought my skull was going to explode.

I suppose I reacted instinctively.

I was still carrying Grandad's spanner, and I held it up to protect myself. The instant it touched the orange circle, there was a dazzling flash, and the spanner flew out of my hand.

But when I glanced upwards, I saw that the orange circle had gone. The globe hadn't, though. It merely paused, as if it were slightly surprised, then started moving forward again.

We hadn't gone very far when a second orange spot appeared. I expected it to change into a circle, like the other one. It didn't. Instead, it grew more and more intense until . . .

It fired an orange bolt at me!

I don't know how I managed to dodge it, but I did. I felt a scorching wave of heat shoot by only millimetres from my cheek, and smelt something burning. The globe had singed my hair!

Now *that* was too close for comfort.

I wasn't going to stand there and let it cook me alive. I fled, dodging and weaving to make myself a more difficult target. I was pretty sure the globe would follow.

I looked over my shoulder once or twice, and

there it was, whisking along noiselessly behind me. Another bolt zipped past my ear, a third just missed my arm . . .

I put on a spurt, but it wasn't going to make much of a difference. My heart sank. A wall was looming in front of me. It went up to the ceiling and down to the floor.

I stopped and scanned it, desperately searching for an exit. There was something, a faint oval outline . . . but if it was a door I certainly couldn't see any way of opening it.

I rested my forehead on the cold metal. My heart was pounding in my chest, and I was completely out of breath. I told myself to calm down, to think. But I knew it was no use.

I was trapped.

I spun round just in time to see the globe come to a halt, less than an arm's length from my face. I watched an orange spot appear, and pressed my back into the wall.

'So much for being the big heroine and saving everybody,' I muttered. I closed my eyes. There was no rule that said I had to watch while I was being fried to a crisp.

But then my fingers found a small rough

patch on the wall. I pressed it, and the oval outline became an opening door. I fell through it, and an orange bolt crackled harmlessly over me.

I jumped to my feet, expecting the globe to follow me. It did, but then stopped just inside the doorway. No orange spots appeared, so I backed away and looked around.

I had tumbled into a circular, shadowed chamber the size of our school hall. In the centre stood a second globe. This one, however, was green – and at least twenty times as big.

It was an incredible sight. A steady glow pulsed deep at its core, while intricate patterns of small lights flowed under the surface like fish chasing each other in the sea.

Similar patterns appeared in the black globe, and suddenly I knew *exactly* what they were doing. They were talking to each other! No, that isn't quite right. They were *arguing*.

A flurry of lights would spread over the green globe, then the black globe would answer. The gaps between got shorter and shorter, and finally both seemed to be talking at once.

At first I was fascinated. But soon I began to

get angry. In the last few minutes I had been terrified, chased, and shot at. And now I was being ignored by a couple of overgrown balloons.

'Excuse *me*,' I said. The globes took absolutely no notice. This calls for stronger measures, I thought. 'HEY!' I shouted as loudly as I could. 'CAN I GET A WORD IN EDGEWAYS?'

The lights vanished so abruptly I was quite startled. But what happened next came as even more of a surprise. New, more complicated patterns appeared on the green globe.

And then it spoke.

'Do you wish to communicate with Om?' it boomed. Its voice was slow and precise, and sounded like some kind of weird synthesizer. It echoed strangely round the chamber.

'I don't know,' I said. 'Who is this . . . Om?'

'I am Om,' said the green globe.

'Why didn't you tell me that in the first place?' I said. 'Er . . . as a matter of act, I *do* want to communicate with you, or whoever's in charge around here.'

'I am in charge,' it said.

'OK,' I said. 'I've got a question for you, and you'd better come up with a pretty good answer. What have you done with my brother? If you've hurt him, I swear I'll . . . '

'Is *brother* the being that resembles you?' said Om.

'Well, some people say we're alike,' I spluttered. 'But I . . . '

'He was collected earlier,' said Om. 'We have prepared him as a sample. We will display him for you.'

I heard a humming noise, and looked into the shadows. Another part of the chamber wall had opened, revealing Luke.

He was standing still, caught in a cone of orange light . . .

11
Questions . . . and Answers

Luke was a statue like the others, his face frozen in a mask of horror. It occurred to me I might have been looking very similar by now if I hadn't brought Grandad's spanner along.

'Is he . . . alive?' I asked.

'Of course,' said Om. I let out a sigh of relief. 'We are very careful to preserve life in the samples we collect. Only thus are they suitable for our purposes.'

'What do you mean, your *purposes*?' I said.

I didn't like the sound of that word at all. My anger was draining away, and my fear was beginning to seep back. I felt very small beside that giant green globe. And very alone.

'You are not entitled to that information,' said Om. 'You and the being known as *brother* are not accounted for. You must explain your presence here.'

'You want *me* to explain . . . ' I said, hardly able to believe what I'd heard. 'You've got to be joking. You're the one who ought to be doing the explaining, not me.'

'That is not possible,' said Om. 'You must respond.'

'*Oh* no,' I said, shaking my head. 'You first. I'm not saying another word until you tell me what's going on.'

Om didn't speak for a while, but it was obviously thinking. Shoals of lights flowed and darted under its surface. It must have told the black globe to go, for it silently slipped out.

'Very well,' said Om at last, making me jump. 'I will answer your questions on one condition. You must also answer mine.'

'Fair enough,' I said. 'Although you've got to tell me everything. Cross your heart and hope to die.'

'Cross your heart . . . hope to die?' said Om, hesitantly. 'Explain, please. My universal translation circuits do not . . . '

'Oh, never mind,' I said. 'Let's just get started. First things first. What sort of creature are you?'

'I am a machine,' it said. 'A computer.'

'I get it,' I said, remembering a science

fiction film I'd seen. 'You're like a giant brain, and you run this spaceship.'

'You are correct,' said Om. 'But how did you know this is. . . '

'Don't interrupt,' I said. 'I haven't finished my turn yet. OK, so you're a computer. Where do you come from?'

'The far side of the galaxy,' said Om. 'I will show you.'

A swirl of black formed deep inside Om, then gradually grew until it filled the whole globe. It was sprinkled with twinkling dots, one of which was bigger than the rest.

'That is our sun,' said Om. 'It has twelve planets, and this craft was sent from the fourth, Gandor.'

'But *who* sent you?' I asked.

'The Slorm,' said Om. 'They are my masters.'

The star-map dissolved and was replaced by the image of a brown planet. Then that faded, and a new picture appeared. It seemed to be a mountain with lots of caves.

We zoomed in closer, and I saw it was really a colossal hive, full of giant, insect-like

creatures. They resembled the machines Luke
and I had encountered in the village.

'Ugh, *yuck*,' I said. 'I hope none of them came
with you.'

'This craft was not designed to carry the
Slorm,' said Om.

'Why did they send *you* here, then?' I said.

'You could call our mission . . . a safety
precaution,' said Om. 'The Slorm have need of
new colonies. We came to see if your planet is
safe for them, before they land here themselves.'

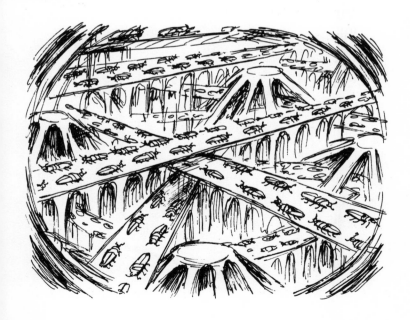

Just as the human race has sent unmanned spacecraft to other planets, so the aliens had sent this ship to explore the Earth. Om had chosen the village because it was isolated.

Like human scientists, the Slorm had programmed their machines to take samples of whatever they found – the air, the soil, and as many living creatures as possible.

That's why the spaceship was full of captured people, including my grandparents and my brother. They were neatly packaged, ready to be transported to Gandor and . . . examined.

That was another word I didn't like the sound of.

'But we don't want a bunch of jumbo alien creepy-crawlies taking us over,' I said. 'And you can't go around kidnapping people. What makes you think you can get away with it?'

'The mission has gone according to plan,' said Om. 'So far there have been only two problems, although the first revealed your planet to be quite dangerous. A probe was destroyed.'

The picture changed to that of a machine drilling into the road. Blue sparks crackled up the rod, and the probe exploded.

'It looks like it hit an underground cable,' I said. So Om hadn't cut off the village's electricity on purpose. That meant it didn't know everything . . . 'What else went wrong?'

'You and the being called *brother* arrived,' said Om.

Now I discovered why Luke and I had been missed. Om explained how the spaceship had passed over the village once to make a list of its potential samples, and pinpoint their positions.

That had been the first shooting star

Grandad had seen. Luke and I had arrived the next day – so we weren't on the list.

The second star had been Om returning. It had jammed the phones and TVs immediately. Then later, it had zapped the whole population with a huge blast of that knockout orange light.

By then Luke and I were in bed. So we missed the machines rustling through the village, somehow opening locked doors and carrying off the people on their list in cocoons of orange energy.

The effect of the orange light on us wore off. We woke up with headaches – and a mystery to solve. But we'd been spotted by the black globe when we'd gone into the village.

Om hadn't known what to make of us at all.

Suddenly I heard a distant clunk, and felt the floor tremble beneath me. A ring of lights appeared round the chamber wall.

'Hey, what's happening?' I asked, nervously.

'I have closed the outer hatch,' said Om. 'The mission has been accomplished. We lift off in two of your Earth minutes . . .'

12
Countdown

One by one the lights round the chamber wall started to flick off. I only realized I was watching a countdown when nearly a quarter of it had already gone. I felt very afraid.

'But wait, you can't take off yet,' I said. 'You . . . you haven't asked me any questions, and it's your turn!'

'I will interrogate you during the voyage to Gandor,' said Om. 'Then you will be prepared as a sample. The observation unit wished to destroy you, but I have forbidden it.'

'Observation unit?' I said, puzzled. 'Oh, you mean the black globe . . . I knew it didn't like me. But listen, er . . . Om, can't we discuss this? You don't seem to understand that . . . '

'Communication will cease during launch sequence,' said Om.

'NO!' I shouted. 'Please, talk to me!'

Om didn't answer. The pictures had disappeared from its interior. It was a silent, pulsing green globe again. And I was completely at its mercy. There was nothing I could do.

Think, I told myself. More lights went, leaving less than half to go. The floor beneath my feet was throbbing now. If only Luke had been more cautious, more like me . . .

Like Om, too, I thought. I had been struck by what it had said about being sent here as a

'safety precaution'. It seemed that everybody was more careful than my brother. Even aliens.

My anger flooded back. The whole thing really bugged me.

Bugged me . . . I stood very still for a second. I had just had the craziest idea. It was so amazing I was sure that if I looked up I would see a big exclamation mark over my head.

I had recalled that conversation between Luke and Grandad in the car. The one about the film in which aliens invaded Earth, but died because they couldn't resist our viruses, our *bugs* . . .

What if I convinced Om that the samples it had collected were a threat to its masters? I nearly smiled. Using Om's own caution to defeat it was something only *I* could think of.

My idea might just work. It had to. There wouldn't be time to come up with anything else. The countdown seemed to be getting faster. Almost three-quarters of the ring of lights had gone.

'I have something very important to tell you, Om,' I said. 'I believe you may be putting your masters . . . in danger.'

My words had an instant effect. The throbbing in the floor changed back to a tremble, then ceased altogether, and the lights stopped disappearing too. There were three left.

'Explain your statement,' boomed Om. At least I've got its attention, I thought. I'd better make this good.

I did, though I do say so myself. I dredged up everything I could remember about the subject of germs and bacteria – especially things like how humans carry them all the time.

I was glad we'd done it recently at school.

'You claim these creatures are invisibly small, but can cause harm, and make other beings sick?' said Om when I'd finished. 'We do not have anything of that nature on Gandor.'

'There you are then,' I said. 'If your masters aren't used to them like us Earthlings, they could get very ill and die. They might even be wiped out. And it would be *your* fault.'

'You are an intelligent life-form,' said Om. 'So this may well be an attempt to trick me. I will therefore examine you and the being known as *brother* for these *germs*.'

A beam of dazzling white light shot out of

Om's centre and hit me. This is it, I thought, and when I looked down, my flesh had become transparent. I could see my entire skeleton!

But it was only the same as having an X-ray, and after a few seconds, the beam shifted to Luke. It seemed to make the strange cone vanish, and Luke's skeleton appeared, just like mine.

'You have spoken the truth,' said Om at last. 'I have detected an extremely high number of micro-organisms in both of you, although the one called *brother* has rather more.'

'That just means he's a typical boy,' I said. 'OK, so now you know. The question is – what are you going to do about it?'

I held my breath and waited while Om thought, lights flashing and winking. This was it, the point of no return – either I had succeeded, or we were going on a one-way trip to the stars.

'I have calculated the possible threat involved,' Om said, eventually. 'And I have decided to unload the samples and fumigate the storage areas. The operation will commence immediately.'

And this time I *did* smile.

Luke didn't, at least, not to begin with. He had come back to life when he was free of the orange light. But he had a splitting headache, and no idea of what was going on.

So I explained everything to him. He stood there looking stupid, and I must admit it gave me a lot of pleasure to know all the answers for once. I was glad he was OK, though.

The black globe returned, probably to get its instructions. In minutes the spaceship was full of bustle and hurry. It reminded me of the station where this whole story had begun.

Machines spun webs of energy round the captives and took them out. Om said the orange light would wear off once the spaceship was safely on its way. Just being careful, I suppose.

Soon Luke was feeling better, and we saw everyone being put back where they belonged. I wondered what I would say to Gran and Grandad. I could hardly believe what had happened myself.

Luke and I watched from the road as the last machine scurried towards the spaceship. Suddenly Luke started to follow it.

'Where do you think you're going?' I said, grabbing his arm.

'My Game Zapper's gone,' he said, showing me his empty back pocket. 'I must have dropped it in there . . .'

'Well, that's where it's staying, then,' I said. 'You could get trapped inside when they leave. It's too risky!'

Luke looked at me . . . and then he grinned.

'OK, Kelly,' he said. 'You're the boss.'

I was so stunned by that, I almost missed the hatch closing and the spaceship taking off. Almost . . . but not quite!